10 9 8 7 6 5 4 3 2 1

Library of Congress Cataloging-in-Publication Data
Birnbaum, Abe, b. 1899.
Green eyes / A. Birnbaum.
p. cm.
Summary: A cat recalls favorite experiences from each season of its
first year of life, from struggling to get out of its cozy box in the spring,
to snuggling by the radiator in the cold of winter.
ISBN 0-307-20203-8 (alk. paper)
1. Cats—Juvenile fiction. [1. Cats—Fiction. 2. Animals—Infancy—Fiction. 3. Seasons—Fiction.]
I. Title. PZ10.3.B536 Gr 2001 [E]—dc21 00-048373

GREEN EYES

A. Birnbaum

 A Golden Book ✦ New York

Golden Books Publishing Company, Inc., New York, New York 10106

My name is Green Eyes. I am an all-white cat with very long whiskers. I am going to have a birthday soon. I will be one year old.

I was born in the country. It was springtime.

When I was very little, I lived in a big wide box with four high walls and a soft pink blanket on the bottom. When the sun was shining, my box was moved outside. The blue sky was my ceiling.

Every day I tried to climb over the walls of my house.
Sometimes my paws would almost reach the top. After
many tries I became stronger. Finally I reached the top
and over I went.

The earth was soft, the grass was green and tall, the flowers had many colors, and the trees were very big.

I ran around and around and around
the biggest tree.

I was tired and happy when
I climbed back into my box.

I remember the first time I saw chickens.

Some were white, some were red, and some were gray.

I also remember the first time I saw dogs and cows and goats.

They all lived on a farm near my house.

Sometimes I would sit and watch the farmer milking the cows. I had a very special reason.

After he unharnessed the horses and fed the pigs,
he would give me a full bowl of warm sweet milk.

During the summer, I was outside most of the time. When it was too hot to play, I would lie down in the tall, cool grass. Once I heard someone say I looked like a little lion in the jungle.

Soon the days became cooler. The leaves turned red and brown

and

fell

slowly

to the

ground.

Sometimes I would choose one leaf and make believe it was a mouse. I would quietly sit and wait for the wind to blow it. Then I would chase it all around the big tree.

The days grew colder and colder, until one day everything was white. It was fun to catch the snowflakes as they fell.

It was too cold to play. My ears were cold, my paws were cold, and my whiskers were covered with snow.

I was glad to lie down in my box near the radiator.

Now it is springtime again.

I am one year old.

I am not a kitten anymore.

I am a cat

and I have a bigger box.

I still like to smell the pretty flowers.

And I like to look at the big trees.

In the summer, I will play in the tall, cool grass.

When autumn comes, I will watch the leaves fall to the ground.

In the winter, I will sit by the window

and watch the snowflakes falling.

And when it gets too cold, I will curl up in my nice warm box

and fall asleep.